KAO KALIA YANG

ILLUSTRATIONS BY

XEE REITER

The Shared Room

University of Minnesota Press
Minneapolis · London

Text copyright 2020 by Kao Kalia Yang
Illustrations copyright 2020 by Xee Reiter

Published by the University of Minnesota Press
111 Third Avenue South, Suite 290
Minneapolis, MN 55401-2520
http://www.upress.umn.edu

Library of Congress Cataloging-in-Publication Data
Names: Yang, Kao Kalia, author. | Reiter, Xee, illustrator.
Title: The shared room / Kao Kalia Yang ; illustrations by Xee Reiter.
Description: Minneapolis : University of Minnesota Press, [2020] |
Audience: Age 8. | Audience: Grades 2-3. | Summary: "A family gradually
moves forward after the loss of a child" —Provided by publisher.
Identifiers: LCCN 2019054494 | ISBN 978-1-5179-0794-5 (hardcover)
Subjects: CYAC: Grief—Fiction. | Family life—Minnesota—Fiction. |
Minnesota—Fiction.
Classification: LCC PZ7.1.Y3648 Sh 2020 | DDC [Fic]—dc23
LC record available at https://lccn.loc.gov/2019054494

Printed in Canada on acid-free paper

The University of Minnesota is an equal-opportunity educator
and employer.

26 25 24 23 22 21 20
10 9 8 7 6 5 4 3 2 1

For the children who miss and grieve and
love those who have gone

For the siblings of Ghia Nah: Ty Lee, Thee Kou,
Dhoua Hli, and the new baby Hlushia,
her sister always and forever

It was a balmy winter day in Minnesota. The sky was heavy with gray clouds. The snow had begun to melt, and patches of yellow grass peeked through the dirty white. The ice grew thin over puddles of dark water and cracked like broken glass.

In an old house on the east side of St. Paul, a mother and father sat before a dark fireplace with their three children playing close by. They kept the light dim in the house. The shadows from the corners reached out and touched the feet of the children.

The light entered the room from a single wide window and a picture on the wall. The window looked out at a red STOP sign where neighborhood children waited for the bus in a long line on school days.

On the wall there was a picture of their fourth child,
another daughter, smiling beneath the summer sun,
her brown hair glinting with streaks of gold,
her eyes soft and shiny, her mouth open in joy,
white teeth in a fine row.

Seven months had passed since the girl in the
picture had drowned.

The day she died had been hot, sweaty. The family had gone to the swimming lake. Bright umbrellas unfolded on sand like flowers in bloom. Elderly people read their newspapers and books on lounge chairs and towels. Young men and women played volleyball nearby.

No one saw the little girl walk
into the water,
laugh when the water touched her toes
with its cool,
walk further into the lake,
feel the water around her waist,
walk until her feet lost touch with
the ground,
float for a moment,
and then struggle to surface.

The day she died now existed as a bubble above all the other days on the family's calendar, a fragile and fierce floating thing, untethered to the earth, well below the clouds but beyond anyone's reach.

Her room had remained empty, her clothes in their drawers, the pictures she had drawn at school still taped on the walls, her bed, her blanket, her sheets, her pillow still held her scent and the dents she had made in them.

Several times each day, the mother or the father opened the door to their daughter's room, went in, sat on the floor beside the bed, leaned their head into the sheets and the blanket, sniffed deep, closed their eyes, and sometimes hoped never to wake again.

But then the three other children called up from the stairs and, no matter how tired, the mother or the father would respond, "I'm coming."

A quiet had entered the house. No matter how loud the boys became, or how hard the younger girl laughed or cried, there seemed a sound barrier over the family. A hush like winter had settled in their home.

Sometimes the quiet got too loud, and the mother and the father played videos of the girl singing on their phones. Her brothers and sister clamored close to watch the image flickering across their screens: a little girl from a happier time laughing and dancing, singing loud, "Let it go, let it go" with her hands raised high above her head, her steps taking her further and further beyond the screen.

The oldest boy was ten. He had shared a room with his younger brother for as long as he could remember. He thought that it would stay like this until everyone grew up and moved away. He did the math: the house had three bedrooms. One bedroom was for the mother and

the father and the baby sister, one was for the sister who had drowned, and the last one was for himself and his brother. He knew old houses didn't grow new rooms easily, and so he believed that he would always share a room with his younger brother.

One warm January day, as he was drawing by himself in the light of the window, his mother said quietly,

"Do you want your sister's room?"

He looked at his parents sitting on low stools before the dark fireplace. His mother was looking at him closely.

He stammered, "Yes."

She said, "Tonight, we'll move you in."

He said, "Where am I going to sleep?"

His father said, "In your sister's bed."

He said, "Where am I going to put my clothes?"

His father answered, "In her drawers."

He had been sad, but he hadn't cried in front of his mother and father. He had comforted his younger brother and sister when they cried. He tried to answer their questions as best he could about where their sister was and why she would never return. Now, the tightness in his chest was climbing up his throat, and no matter how hard he swallowed he knew it would erupt.

His next words came out in a cry and a question: "She's never coming back?"

His hands covered his eyes and his face so all he saw was the water of his world spilling over in the dark of his closed palms.

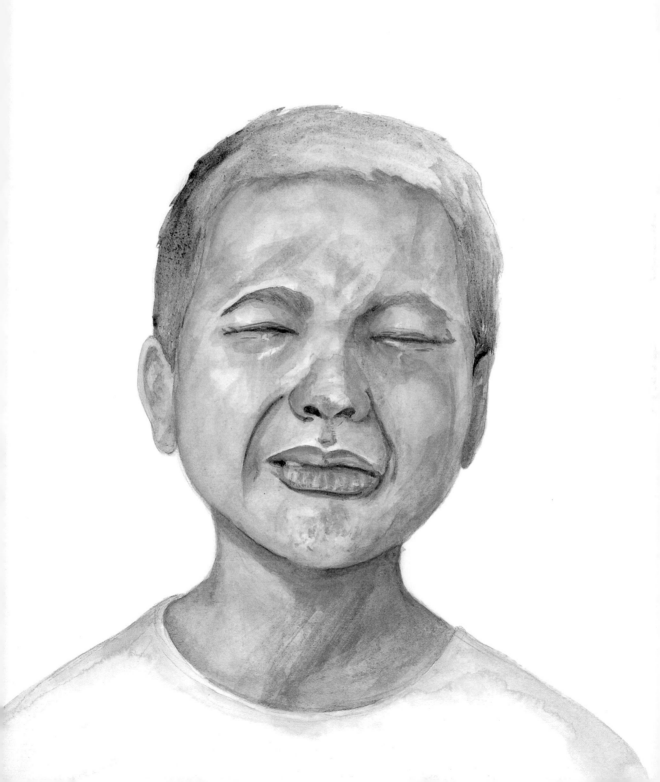

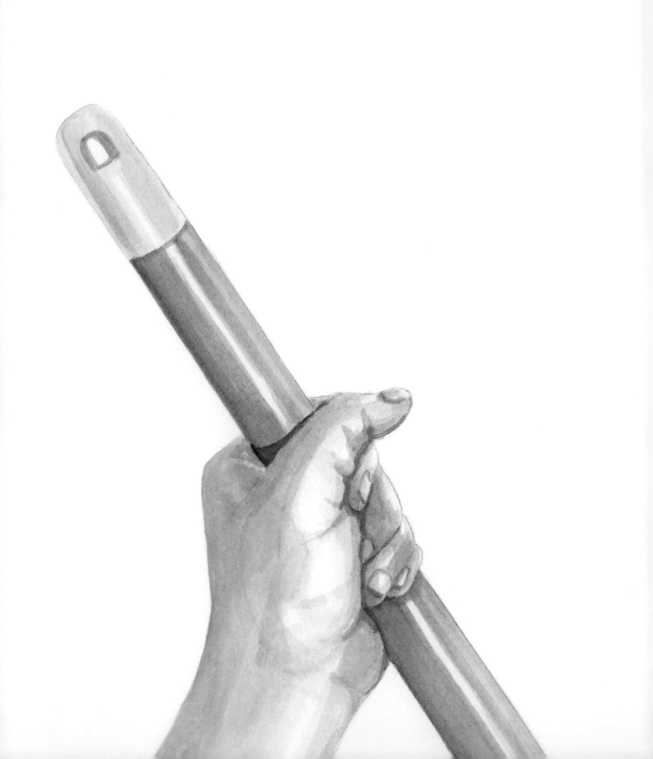

That night, the mother and the father and the boy took off the sheets from the sister's bed and put on new sheets. His mother went through her daughter's drawers and folded the clothes into an empty suitcase for her younger girl to wear in a couple of years. His father swept the room with a broom and the girl's hair stuck on its tip. With his hands he pulled her hair out from the bristles, and he held the dust and the strands of light hair tight in his palm.

That night the big brother slept in his new room. He could see the neighborhood through his new window, and he saw how the world had looked to his sister from her place of rest: peaceful.

Later that evening, a winter storm blew in on the waves of the warm winds that had visited. Outside, the snow fell lightly at first, becoming increasingly heavy beneath the dark cover of night until the flakes grew so thick that the streetlamps disappeared from view.

In the morning, the old house on the east side of St. Paul was covered in snow, and the family inside huddled close to their fireplace, now alight with flames, keeping each other warm, their little girl's memory like the fire before them, a melt in the freeze of their hearts.

Kao Kalia Yang is the author of the children's book *A Map into the World*, as well as the award-winning books *The Song Poet* and *The Latehomecomer: A Hmong Family Memoir*, a National Endowment for the Arts Big Read title. She lives with her family in St. Paul, Minnesota.

Xee Reiter is a first-generation Hmong American artist and illustrator. She lives in St. Paul with her husband and three children.